JOY OF THE SEASON

HEATHER SCARLETT

If this Grinch in a cowboy hat thinks he can steal Joy's Christmas spirit, he's got another thing coming.

No one believes in the magic of Christmas more than Joy Williams. She owns a Christmas-themed store in Wildwood Falls, Montana, and loves nothing more than sharing the happiness of the holidays with her customers. But then a sexy cowboy saunters into town, with his fancy boots, shiny belt buckle, and lazy smile—and an eviction notice. Turns out, he's her new landlord, and his plans for the building don't include her shop.

Luke Hudson is a down-on-his-luck ex-rodeo star. After a devastating injury caused him to miss out on the rodeo circuit for a full season, he needs an infusion of cash—fast. When he unexpectedly inherits an historic building, the solution is clear. Evict the tenants and sell the building. But after meeting the charming owner of the Christmas shop, that's easier said than done.

It'll take more than Christmas magic to save Joy's store and teach Luke the importance of community. They'll both have to lay their hearts on the line.

CHAPTER 1

Joy Williams stepped out onto Main Street, holding her peppermint mocha, and reveling in the holiday decorations. Two years of living in Wildwood Falls, Montana, had not dampened her holiday spirit one bit. She loved the over the top decorations that lined the wide downtown street the moment midnight struck on Thanksgiving. *This town was made for holidays.*

She smiled at familiar faces as she made her way to her store. Glancing across the street, she was pleased to note that the large Christmas tree in the center of town was being decorated. One of her favorite events was the annual tree lighting on Christmas Eve.

The crisp morning air bit her cheeks as she fumbled with her key in the lock to her store, Tinsel & Co. Damn gloves. No amount of years living in winter climate would make her more graceful while wearing winter gloves. She didn't care, though. Moving to Montana was a dream come true. There may be a few times in the dark winter days of January when she wondered why she had given up Florida for a snowy climate, but today was not one of those days.

Today was the official start of the holiday season. Black Friday. She had long days ahead of her these next few weeks in the shop. She couldn't wait. The look of wonder in her customer's eyes as they entered her shop and took in all the holiday decorations was magical. Wildwood Falls attracted a good amount of tourists in the winter thanks to the nearby ski mountain. And all of them stopped at her store, located in the most historic building in town. Whether to buy a souvenir or bring their children for cookies and cocoa story time, they came by the droves. The holidays were her thing.

She stowed her coat and purse in the back room, flicking the switch that played holiday music, filling the store with familiar classics. Surveying her store from this vantage point, Joy took a deep breath and smiled. She couldn't imagine life being any more perfect than this moment.

She stood near the large window, sipping her mocha, watching people walk to and from various shops. She had learned to take breaks when they came, as they were few and far between this time of year.

A tall cowboy striding purposely down the other side of the street caught her attention. He stopped nearly opposite her store. He was striking. Tall, lean. *Dangerous.* His cowboy hat was pulled low so she couldn't see his face. His whole demeanor screamed trouble. From his tight wranglers to his fitted jacket. He looked like a man of action. *Who was he?*

He looked across the street, seeming to sense her appraisal, meeting her eyes through the picture window. She jumped at the contact, nearly dropping her drink. Finding her composure, she quickly backed out of view and set her coffee on the counter.

Risking a glance back, she saw he was headed her way. Butterflies danced in her stomach. *What did a handsome cowboy want with her Christmas shop?*

She busied herself arranging merchandise near the register, pretending that she was totally fine with this new development. It wasn't that she didn't have the occasional cowboy in her shop, but not usually early in the day. Ranch work was an early business.

The chime above the door rang, announcing his arrival. Joy pushed down her nerves and turned with a sunny smile.

"Merry Christmas!" It was her standard greeting this time of year.

The cowboy regarded her for a long moment before offering a reply.

"Morning." The words sounded scraped over hot coals. He didn't qualify with good morning, simply morning. An observation on the state of things. Not a greeting per se.

Irritation rose, but Joy tamped it down. There was no room for irritation in Tinsel & Co.

"Can I help you find something? A gift maybe?"

"No, I'm just looking around."

Joy shrugged, which was a very un-Joy-like gesture, and returned to fussing over her decor. Something about this cowboy grated. Maybe it was because he didn't exude pure happiness at her artful arrangements throughout the store. He retained his scowl as he looked around. One did not scowl at perpetual Christmas cheer.

Clearly not having received the memo, the handsome cowboy stood in her entryway, scowling at the elaborate decor that took her a whole summer to design.

"Who owns this place?"

Joy jumped at the sudden question. Mysterious cowboy was a man of few words, but when he spoke, he knew how to command a room.

"I own this store."

His shocked eyes met hers and a feeling of dread crawled up her spine.

"Well, I own the building. And, I'm here to evict you."

CHAPTER 2

Luke felt like the Scrooge. He walked into the most beautiful Christmas store he had ever seen, owned by the most beautiful woman he had ever seen, and dropped a bomb. He hated to do it the way he did, but direct was always best, no matter how painful. He had learned that lesson the hard way.

Luke felt sharp sting of directness when the doctor told him he would never be able to return to the rodeo circuit after his bad fall last season. He had worked hard to prove him wrong. Money had been the final obstacle. Inheriting this building allowed him to clear the last hurdle to return to work and repay his family for shelter, food, and medical bills the past 6 months.

"Excuse me?" The only tell she gave that she'd heard him the first time was her pale face and panicked eyes. With a blink, her eyes became cool and distant. Two bright spots of color developed on her pale cheeks.

Please don't make me say it again.

"You're planning to evict me." She straightened to her full height, which he estimated to be 5'7".

He was struck by her lithe figure. She had a dancer's body, with long limbs and strong, lean muscle. He shook his head to clear it. This was no time to be thinking of her attractiveness. *In another situation, I might ask her out.* This was not that kind of situation, though. The coolness in her eyes had given way to banked anger. If she could strike him down on the spot, she would do it gladly.

Gone was the cheer she had exuded moments before. He waited for the inevitable explosion, but it didn't come.

"Who are you, anyway?" Her voice was strained and sounded like she was holding back tears. *Don't cry. I don't know what to do with tears.*

"I'm Luke Hudson. My family owns a ranch outside town."

"And, you own this building." The pitch of her voice inched higher. "Why am I just finding this out now? And why do you want to evict me?"

"I just inherited this property last week from my Great Aunt Mary. And, it's not just you. It's the whole building. I'm planning to sell it. I have some interest from a developer who wants to convert the building to condos."

"Condos! This building is historic. It's the oldest one in Wildwood Falls. It can't be turned into…condos." Her nose scrunched in disgust.

"Don't worry, you'll have plenty of time to find a new location. We won't be breaking ground until spring." Guilt punched him in the gut. He reminded himself that he needed the money from the sale if he had any hope of returning to the rodeo circuit.

She shook her head, her bright blond locks swinging with the movement.

"Your Aunt Mary would never have wanted you to sell."

Then why did she leave it to him? His Aunt knew he wasn't one to stay around his hometown.

He realized he never got her name.

"What's your name?"

Surprised by the question, she pursed her lips in a frown before responding. "I'm Joy." "Joy? Like the joy of the season?" Did you open a Christmas store because of your name?"

Joy rolled her eyes at his admittedly ridiculous question.

He shrugged. "Had to be asked."

"Actually, it didn't. Luke. Rancher, historic building owner, investigative journalist."

"Don't forget award-winning bull rider." He gave a wry smile.

She stuck out her hand to shake. "Joy. Christmas shop owner, named after holiday cheer, and newly evicted."

CHAPTER 3

Luke's handshake was firm and warm. She brushed off the tingles she felt at his touch. *Must be stress.* She certainly couldn't be attracted to the man who just turned her life upside down.

The bell over the door chimed as a customer entered. They both jumped, startled by the interruption. She turned to greet the customer, but Luke touched her arm.

"Please, there's just one more thing."

Joy indicated to the customer she would be one more minute and turned back to Luke.

"There was a condition in the will."

"Condition?" What kind of condition could there possibly be?

"My Great Aunt…wanted me to get to know the downtown district a little better before I inherit the title."

"Ok…." Joy looked puzzled.

"I'm supposed to join the downtown chamber's holiday committee and participate in the events on Main St." He paused, shifting his feet before continuing. "I'm supposed to help with the chamber's signature events…the annual tree lighting and the…"

"The Holiday Lights Stroll," Joy guessed. Those were the biggest holiday events in Wildwood Falls.

"Yes, once I participate in the committee and complete the holiday season, then her lawyer will transfer the deed to my name."

"I see."

"Yes, so like I said, it will be a little while before you'll have to find a new space. I have to wait essentially until Christmas to inherit the property."

Joy nodded her understanding. This was an unusual stipulation. Why would his Great Aunt Mary set that requirement?

"Do you happen to know who I can contact about joining the committee?" He had the courtesy to look sheepish. He didn't spend much time in Wildwood Falls or he would know that information.

"Yes. You want to contact me. I chair the committee."

Of course, she was the chair of the holiday committee. Joy, whose name perfectly fits her store and her personality would certainly be the person chairing the most important committee in Wildwood Falls. He didn't know much about what was going on in town, but he knew this committee, and the events they planned, was the pride and joy of the downtown district.

"I see. How lucky I started here first." He ducked his head and stared at the vintage floor tiles. "I'd like to join the committee."

Looking up, he met her eyes, which were the prettiest

blue he'd ever seen. The color of the ocean. Currently, the color of a stormy ocean.

"I don't know if that's possible. Our committee has already done most of the planning for this holiday season. I'm not sure there's much more we need."

And, of course, she was going to make him beg. He supposed he should expect nothing less, given how he barged in and dropped this bomb on her.

"I'll jump in and do anything you all need. Seriously, no job is too big or too small."

"And, you need to jump these hoops to inherit the property."

"Yes, that's right."

"And, if it wasn't for the stipulation in the will, you wouldn't be volunteering your time."

"Yes, true again." He usually wasn't in Wildwood Falls during the holidays long enough to get involved.

"Give me one reason why I should nominate you to the committee."

Damn. He supposed *because I need you to* wasn't going to fly. Luke racked his brain to think of a compelling reason.

"I have a connection to someone who makes handcrafted nutcrackers. They would be a great item to feature at the auction. They would bring in a lot of money for the children's charity."

He wasn't sure that would buy him entry, but he hoped it would. Joy must care about the local children's charity that the auction raised money for. Hopefully her care for the charity would outweigh her dislike for him. In recent years, he knew from his Mom's reports that the auction had struggled to bring in enough crafts to raise the desired dollar amount.

Sure enough, the light in Joy's eyes shifted from stormy ocean to summer day.

"Nutcrackers? And, you're sure this person would be willing to donate?"

"Absolutely." He hoped his brother, Cameron, would be agreeable to this plan. He was sure he would be once he explained the charity aspect.

Joy frowned slightly, seeming to think over his proposal.

"Alright, you can join. We meet Tuesday at 6 p.m. at Town Hall. Don't be late."

With that, she turned away and moved towards her customer, leaving Luke in her wake.

CHAPTER 4

Joy turned off the holiday music, feeling relieved. Today had been a day. She was so rattled by Luke's announcement he planned to sell her building that she could scarcely concentrate the rest of the day. It wasn't just her business at stake, it was her home. She rented one of the four apartments in the building and had a commute of 30 seconds. Beyond that, she could afford the rent.

What was she going to do when she had to pay full market value rent in Wildwood Falls and find an apartment she could afford? That seemed near impossible since the town had become a larger tourist attraction than ever and rents for both businesses and apartments were at a premium.

She considered canceling her dinner plans with her friends, Sarah and Rylee. She felt too guilty, though to do it. A single Mom, Rylee had arranged for childcare for her son and was looking forward to a rare night out. And, Sarah worked just as hard as her as the sole proprietor of her coffee business on the corner of the historic building.

Resigned, Joy headed down the street to the local restaurant where they had agreed to meet.

She saw Rylee as soon as she rounded the corner.

"Rylee!" she greeted her friend with more enthusiasm than usual. It was so nice to see a familiar face after her day.

Rylee smiled when she spotted Joy. She reached to hug her. "How was your day? Busy I'm sure."

Rylee nodded. "Busy is an understatement. More like life-changing."

Noting her frown, Rylee squeezed her shoulder. "Let's sit down and you can tell me all about it." Sarah joined them moments later and the group headed inside to be seated. Joy proceeded to tell her friends about her interaction with Luke today.

Rylee frowned. "Luke. I know that name. My older brother went to high school with him. His family has been in Wildwood Falls for generations."

She paused to chew a breadstick. "I don't get what he'd want with that building, though. Why sell out to an outsider?"

Joy shrugged. "I have no idea, but he's costing me my business and my home."

"We can't stand for that, now can we?"

"What am I supposed to do?

"Well, you fight back. "

Joy shook her head. "That's not my style."

"Oh, so losing your home and business is your style?"

Thinking of how hard it was to move here and start the business, Joy shook her head. "No, I don't want to lose it."

"Well, then," Rylee said decisively. "You're gonna need to fight for it."

Fight for it.

Joy went to bed that night with the mantra in her mind. *Fight for it.* She couldn't think of a time she'd fought for anything. Conflict was something she avoided at all costs. If there was a time to embrace conflict, though, this was it.

The next morning, she woke with a renewed determination to save the building. She realized she wasn't the only one who had something to lose if the building was sold. The other tenants had businesses and homes on the line. The building had been a fixture in town for 100 years. The whole town would lose a piece of its history if the building sold to an outsider.

With renewed resolve, Joy hatched a plan. A few visits to her fellow tenants before she opened her store garnered support.

In her few years in Wildwood Falls, she had gotten to know a lot of people. She had become part of the fabric of the town. Much more than Luke, who rumor had it, spent the better part of his past decade on the rodeo circuit raising hell.

Opening her store that morning, sipping her peppermint mocha, Joy smiled to herself. Within 24 hours, she had gone from victim to heroine of her story.

CHAPTER 5

For the second day in a row, Luke found himself driving down Main St., finding parking on the decorative main drag. This time, his business was at the cafe on the corner of his new building. *His building.* He still couldn't wrap his head around the idea that he owned real estate. Lucrative real estate at that. He had a meeting with a realtor who planned to list the property. Rather than meet at his ranch, he chose to meet downtown. The longer he avoided his family finding out, the better. His family was as old as the town and older than the building he inherited. He didn't think his brothers would much care what he did with it, but his Mom sure would. He hoped to avoid that uncomfortable conversation as long as possible.

He was early, so he ordered a cup of black coffee and settled into a seat in the corner, idly flipping through that morning's edition of the local paper. *Who reads this drivel?* He thought to himself as he flipped past local gossip and news of local politics. A full-page ad caught his attention. A large, color picture of the historic building, *his building*. The text read *Save a Wildwood*

Falls Historic Landmark. The ad went on to explain that it was being sold to outside investors and would be destroyed, along with the town's history. It gave a date and time for a meeting for all interested parties to attend. Luke nearly growled his frustration. So much for a quick sale and a return to the circuit. It seemed the pretty blond wouldn't go down without a fight. Little did she know that Luke gave as good as he got.

His realtor arrived, busying herself with plans of how to list the site and arranging to take key pictures to best showcase the building. The realtor indicated she had already had interest just based on the ad in this morning's paper. So maybe this would end up working to his advantage. Satisfied with the plan, Luke said goodbye to the realtor and headed to Tinsel & Co. He had a very good idea of who had placed that ad.

Pushing open the door to the quaint shop, he felt a twinge of guilt that he would put it out of business. *She can find another place to rent.* Wildwood Falls is a tourist mecca, after all. He ignored the guilt and proceeded into the shop, which had transformed into an even more over the top holiday experience if that were possible. How had she managed to make an already festive holiday shop even more Christmas-y in the past few days?

Joy looked up with a start from where she was wrapping a gift for a customer. She met his eyes and his stomach dropped, the feeling almost visceral.

Nodding his head in greeting, he proceeded to wander around the store, looking at the various items for sale. He stopped in front of a display of RC trains, set around a small track that was operational. He toggled the switch and the train chugged to life, the cars making their way around the display area. There was even a flatbed train with a collection of Christmas trees, which reminded him of his friend, Eric, who owned a Christmas tree farm. The attention to detail was astounding.

A sound behind him alerted him to Joy's presence. Turning, he took in her dark rinse jeans, red sweater, and black flats.

"Hello, Luke." She turned wary eyes on him. Did she know he saw the ad? Luke shook off his paranoia. He was just here for a friendly visit to find out what the heck she was thinking of placing a full page ad calling him out.

He knew. There was no other explanation as to why he would be here, in her store, mere days after notifying her of eviction, unless he had seen the ad. She hadn't expected him to be the type to read a local paper so figured it would be a few days before he would get wind of her plan.

She waited for him to drop the bomb that he knew or have harsh words for her. Instead, he just watched her, with that sharp gaze. She would have preferred he yell. His gaze, raking over her, assessing her, was unsettling. She would not be the first to break the silence, though.

Finally, Luke did. "How's business?" That was not what she expected.

She glanced at him warily. "It's good. This is always my best season."

"I like the train set up." The compliment, as well as the change of topic, caught her off guard. Did he like her store?

"Thanks. Can't have Christmas without trains."

"I guess not. I always liked mine under the tree when I was a kid."

"Yes, little boys love trains."

"I'm not a little boy anymore." No, he wasn't, Joy thought as she took in the muscles bulging beneath his ribbed henley shirt. He was one prime specimen of a man. A man that's evicting you, she chided herself.

"I have something for everyone in the store. For girls, boys, parents. Every year I pick out new items but always keep the old favorites. So, parents and grandparents can come shop and remember the magic of their Christmas growing up."

His gaze swept the store. "Yes, it seems you do."

"This is more than a tourist trap. This store is…home. For me and my staff and the regulars from the town who come in year-round."

Luke seemed to consider that as he continued to gaze around the store.

"A little bit of home in Wildwood Falls, Montana?" he asked with a wistful edge to his voice.

"Yes, something like that. Not all of us are from here, but we've made our home here."

He nodded, seeming to consider that.

"It's funny. I spent my life trying to get out of a place someone else wants to be a part of. I like what you've done with the store. You'll be able to move to a different space, I'm sure. After the holidays is probably the best time to relocate. You'll be ready for tourists before the spring thaw."

"This town, this store, is my world. I can't imagine not being a part of the town."

Why hadn't he mentioned the ad?

"It may be strange to offer, given the circumstances, but if you need any help finding a new space, let me know. My family knows everyone in town. I wouldn't be above pulling a favor if it helped you."

The offer warmed Joy's heart. She couldn't help thinking about what would happen if they hadn't met under such awkward circumstances. Would they have hit it off? Become friends? Dated? No sense wishing for things that were not to be.

"Thank you. It would be easier to just not sell. Then nothing would have to change."

Luke sighed, running his hand through his hair. "The thing is, I need the money. I got hurt pretty bad last rodeo season and need the money. I was out of work and my family supported me, including paying medical bills I couldn't afford. I need to pay them back. I lost my sponsorship so need to pay my own way into the season. I have no other way except to sell."

Joy could see the pain on Luke's face as he talked. She understood the desire to make one's own way in the world. And being dependent on others was tough. She understood but that didn't make it any easier.

"I get it, I just wish it were different."

"Yeah, me too. I guess I should go." Luke started to leave, turning back to her at the last moment. "Oh, and Joy?"

"Yes?"

"Your ad won't change my mind."

With that pronouncement, he walked out the door, shutting it so firmly behind him the bell jangled precariously.

CHAPTER 6

Luke pulled up the long driveway leading to his family's ranch, a lead weight in his stomach. He dreaded large family dinners and knew this one would be especially bad. He knew his family would have seen the local paper by now and know he was planning to sell out. He had seriously considered making an excuse to get out of dinner but figured it was best to just get it over with.

He parked and walked into the cozy great room of his family's ranch. A fire burning in the large fireplace that dominated one wall of the great room. The great room was two stories and while it should be imposing, it was very homey.

Today, it was less cozy than usual. The large fireplace couldn't chase the chill emanating from his mother when he walked into the room.

"Hello, Mom."

"Don't hello me."

He turned his best *what did I do* look at her. The one that had worked when he was a teenager.

"Don't look at me like that. You know exactly what I'm talking about."

He sighed. "You saw the paper then?"

"The whole town saw the paper. What were you thinking? Telling those good people who have rented for years that you were going to sell right out from under them?!"

"They have plenty of notice, Mom, to find other places to lease. It's not like I'm throwing them out in the cold."

His Mom sniffed. "You might as well. The more popular the town has become with tourists, the higher the leases go. There is just nothing reasonably affordable in downtown now. Not for the little local owned shops."

Luke bristled. He was a grown man. He didn't need his Mom giving him a lecture on how he was going to manage his inheritance. "It will be fine, Mom. I need the money to go back out on the circuit. Last season was a bust." His bad spill last year had cost him the better part of the season. To come back now, he needed some serious capital.

"Those tenants are people, Luke. Citizens of this town. You can't just up and sell out from under them."

"So, you're on their side, are you?"

His Mom rolled her eyes in exasperation. "I'm not on any side, Luke. But, you were raised in this town and used to be a part of this community. I'd think you would have a better sense of right and wrong when it came to this property."

As always, she had that Mom's way of making him feel guilty when he shouldn't. No, he shouldn't feel guilty. He had a right to do what he needed with the building. As soon as he jumped the hoops his Aunt had stipulated. He needed to get back to the rodeo. He really couldn't see another way.

Heading to the kitchen to escape further maternal guilt trips, he snagged a beer from the fridge and greeted his brother.

He took a moment to tell his youngest brother, Cameron,

about the holiday auction and secure his agreement to make some of his nutcrackers for the event. Cameron worked the ranch with Luke's other two brothers, but always enjoyed the opportunity to let his creative side shine.

His brother William, who had taken over the responsibility of running the ranch, pulled him aside after dinner.

"Sorry Mom was so hard on you. I know you're doing what you think you need to do."

Luke gave Will an assessing stare. "I'm doing what I know I need to do."

"Well, that's what I want to talk to you about. I have an idea of something else you could do."

Luke was skeptical. "I only know the rodeo. I suck at school, don't want to tie myself down to a 9-5. I'm not cut out to be a rancher like you. So, rodeo it is."

"Rodeo is involved in my idea. I think you'd be great at training horses for the rodeo. I just bought a few horses. Thought I'd try my hand at breeding."

"That's a good idea. Good money if you know what you're doing."

William nodded. "That was what I was thinking. One of the horses clearly won't work as a breeding horse. Too spunky, but smart as all get out. I was thinking it would be a great rodeo horse."

Luke took a thoughtful sip of his beer. "Okay, but I don't see where I come into this."

Will grinned. "You know horses. You know rodeo. You know what it takes to make it there. You'd know exactly how to train a horse for the rodeo."

Luke's initial reaction was a flat out rejection of his older brother's suggestion.

"No way. I ride in the rodeo. I'm not ready to hang up my hat and retire to be a trainer."

Will shrugged as if it meant nothing to him one way or

another. "Think about it. It could be a great way to have a steady income and stay in Wildwood Falls."

"I'm not planning to stay here, Will."

His brother shrugged again. "Just saying, if you decide you want to stay, the job offer stands."

The buzz around the large table stopped cold as soon as Luke walked in. A bevy of women stared in open-mouthed shock as he pulled a chair and sat down. They all looked to the head of the table where Joy sat, slowly sipping one of those fancy coffees she so obviously loved. The room was poised for her reaction. The women would take her lead in how to react to this most unwelcome development.

Luke found himself holding his breath, waiting as well. Stop acting like a schoolboy, he chided himself. You're a grown man who faces angry bulls regularly. The holiday committee is no sweat to you.

Joy assessed the group before speaking, meeting each pair of cautious eyes with a seemingly unspoken message. Luke watched the table relax by increments as her gaze made its way around. She then turned her attention to him.

"Luke, welcome to the holiday committee. Thank you for accepting my invitation."

She didn't add that the invitation was requested from him as a condition from his aunt. Surprised that she wouldn't take this opportunity to take him down a notch, Luke offered his best cowboy charm to the group.

"Pleased to be here. Growing up in Wildwood Falls, I've always looked forward to the holiday traditions.

A woman with gray hair that looked familiar spoke up. "Luke, I've known you since you were a boy. And I've gotta say, I'm disappointed in you. Selling the building to outsiders..."

She was cut off by a look and shake of Joy's head. "Miss Velma, no need to bring up that unpleasantness here. We're here to bring holiday cheer to the town and that is what we'll do. The rest will handle itself."

With that pronouncement, she proceeded to lead them through the agenda, which involved much about decor, events, and logistics. Luke's head spun by the end of it. He had no idea so much work and planning went into the downtown holidays. He found his thoughts drifting to his childhood memories of holidays in Wildwood Falls.

"....Luke and I will judge the holiday lights contest." Joy closed her binder with a snap and brought the meeting to a close. Holiday lights contest? He didn't remember that from his childhood. He considered asking Joy but then he'd have to admit he wasn't paying attention. No good giving her a reason to kick him off the committee.

He exited the room with the rest of the group, all of whom were planning to meet up for treats at the bakery next door. No one invited him. His chest felt suddenly tight, which must be the cold night air. Luke was not the joining type. Never had been. Even on the rodeo circuit, he showed his face at the bars after the show, staying on the fringes of the group. He occasionally found himself a like-minded companion for the evening, but not nearly as much as the other rodeo cowboys.

He turned to face Joy, whose cheeks had turned an adorable shade of pink in the cold. How could someone so sweet-looking be plotting to ruin him?

CHAPTER 7

Why had she gone and assigned Luke to the holiday lights contest, which was her signature holiday event? When she took over the committee a few years ago, the town was losing interest in the holiday festivities that had been the same for more years than anyone could count. Determined to engage the young people of the town, she started the holiday lights contest. It was new and fresh and there was a cash prize. The response was overwhelming and the tradition had grown so popular that many of the downtown streets rivaled the neon of Las Vegas during the holidays. It was her favorite event. And she had just asked Luke to share it with her.

For his part, she wasn't sure he even realized he was invited. He was checked out in the meeting, furthering her resolve to prevail in her fight to save her building. She chalked the invite up to working on him with any angle possible, including playing on his soft side (if he had one). Who could resist holiday lights?

She was coming to regret having committed to hours of walking around a dark downtown with a man whose attractiveness was positively lethal in the glow of holiday lights. Handsome, his cut jaw highlighted by the white lights on the window he was standing in front of. Eyes glittering with something she couldn't name but sent shivers down her back. Must be the cold.

"I'll walk you to your car." Luke, a gentleman? She hadn't expected that. Her heart lurched and the protective layer over it cracked just a bit.

"This is Wildwood Falls. I'm hardly at risk walking a block down Main St."

Luke offered a crooked grin. "Maybe it's for my protection. Bears scare me." He winked and Joy felt another crack in her protective shield. This would not do.

"Bears hibernate in winter, Luke" She couldn't help but return his smile. Damn, he was charming.

They walked in silence down the empty block. The familiar sound of snow crunching under her boots soothed her. The air was still and she could feel snowflakes softly land on her nose. Looking up, she reveled in the soft snow that had begun to fall. The snow was magical. Growing up in Florida, she never experienced winter. Now, it was her favorite season.

She turned her face up to the falling snow, reveling in the sensation.

A light dusting gathered on the sidewalk and surrounding buildings. This wouldn't be a big storm, just enough to freshen up the town with a fresh coat of powder. She turned to find Luke watching her curiously.

Their eyes met and held for a long moment. Joy looked away first, with a shake of her head. No time for intense cowboys in her life. She had holiday magic to create. What was that saying? Those who couldn't do, taught? She brushed off the thought. Just because she hadn't had a significant relationship didn't mean she couldn't. It just meant she was extremely picky. Rodeo cowboys certainly did not make the cut.

Why did he agree to this nonsense? Because he needed to as a condition of his inheritance. Stuffing his hands in his pockets to keep warm, he bounced on his heels waiting for Joy to lock her shop for the evening. Tonight was the judging for the holiday lights contest. She had a clipboard in hand with the addresses and rating sheets. Very official. Her blond hair was long and wavy tonight, contrasting with the cheery red of her coat.

"Ready?"

Luke gestured to the sidewalk and she took the lead to the first house. They stood in front of the small home, which was bedecked with multicolor lights, complete with a Santa's workshop in the front yard. The animated figures moved to a holiday tune and Luke once again questioned his life choices. How was he qualified to judge this?

"How cute!" Joy's eyes lit up as she watched the show. She paused to take a few notes on her clipboard before moving down the street. They walked several blocks, seeing countless holiday displays, before circling back to Main St.

"I have to admit, I wasn't sure what to expect, but that was enjoyable," Luke surprised himself at how much fun he had taking in all the festive lights.

"Oh, we're not done yet! We have at least four more blocks to judge."

"Four blocks?!" Holiday light contests were not for the faint of heart. Luke glanced towards the tents set up to serve visitors to the holiday lights display. "We need sustenance if we have so much left to see." He steered Joy towards the tent serving hot chocolate. He ordered two, with all the fixings, and passed one to Joy.

"Thank you, Luke." Was that a blush? He was struck once again by her beauty in the crisp winter air. This climate suited her. They spent a few minutes around the bonfire drinking their hot chocolate before resuming their task.

The last street of the contest had created an archway of white lights, with a sprig of mistletoe in the center. "Oh, how delightful!" Joy stepped into the center and twirled around.

A passerby stopped. "Let me take a picture of you two under the mistletoe. It will make such a pretty picture."

Joy froze and started to decline. Luke looked between the older man and Joy. What was the harm of a quick picture? The older gentleman looked so excited.

"Sure, thanks," Luke answered for them and moved to step next to Joy. He took her clipboard and handed it off to the passerby along with his phone. Putting his arm around Joy, he set his face next to hers as the camera snapped a pic.

"Ok, now a kiss. You *are* under the mistletoe after all."

Luke turned to kiss Joy on the cheek.

"C'mon now. You can do better than that. Give your girl a proper kiss. It's a holiday tradition."

Joy started to correct the older gentleman that they were not a couple. Before she could get the words out, Luke leaned in close. "One quick kiss? For tradition."

Joy nodded and Luke leaned in. They stayed suspended in the moment for what seemed like an eternity. The delicious moment before a first kiss. Surprising him, Joy leaned in to close the distance and their lips met.

Sparks. That was the only way he could describe the kiss. Sweet, chaste, but setting off enough sparks to blaze through the night. Luke had always thought of fanciful descriptions to be fairy tales. He'd certainly never experienced anything like this. Joy put her fingers to her lips, looking dazed, her eyes wide with shock. Had she felt it too?

He accepted his phone back from the older gentleman with a nod of thanks. Joy still hadn't moved from her spot under the mistletoe. Impulsively, he snapped a pic of her. Now he'd always have the memory of her struck by his kiss, touching her lips reverently while she gazed into the distance.

The flash of the camera phone seemed to snap her out of her reverie. "Ok, enough fun. We have to get back to business. We still have a few more houses left to judge."

They reached the end of judging and found themselves standing in front of her store.

"Do you need help calculating the scores?"

"I'll do that tomorrow evening. Thank you for your help, Luke. Have a good night." The primness in her voice was such a contrast to her usual cheerfulness, that Luke felt dismissed and turned to walk away, first making sure she was safely inside.

CHAPTER 8

What kind of crazy magical spell had she fallen under? She was still dazed by Luke's kiss. It wasn't as if she hadn't been kissed before. Something about that kiss, though, had shaken her to her core. It must be the mistletoe and romance of the holiday setting. It certainly couldn't be Luke.

Distraction. That was her best defense. She had hustled them through the rest of the displays, pretending to give each her rapt attention.

She was still thinking about Luke when she got home. As she got ready for bed. Before she fell asleep. And the next morning, that kiss was the first thing on her mind. She threw herself into her work, which was easy during the holiday rush. She worked all day, barely coming up for air or a snack. Before she knew it, it was 6 o'clock. Closing time. She turned the lock on the door, dimmed the lights in the shop, and slumped against the counter. After a momentary allowance of being human, she straightened and pulled the file of judging slips out. She really should calculate the points before she went home.

A knock on the door startled her and she looked up, only to see Luke standing there, looking every bit the sexy rodeo star he was. He smiled and held up a bag of some kind. Getting closer, she realized it was a takeout bag from the local gourmet shop. Luke brought her dinner? She unlocked the door and let him in.

"What's this?"

He looked sheepish. Was that a blush? "I thought you'd need dinner since you're staying late to tabulate scores from the contest."

She stepped back, indicating he should pass through into the store. She locked the door behind them and turned to see him heading to the back of the store. He stopped at the small sitting area with several wing chairs and a faux fireplace, complete with stockings hung on the mantle. He placed the bags on a low table between the chairs and pulled out various items. First, he pulled out several kinds of cheese, then crackers, olives, and cured meats. He opened packages and arranged them on the table. A few more items appeared, including individual desserts. Joy's mouth watered and her stomach growled, loudly. She was famished, it turned out.

Luke's laugh seemed to warm the space. "I see you appreciate the spread," he remarked, pulling a final item out of his magic bag of tricks. A bottle of red wine. "I hope you like Pinot Noir. The store owner said it went well with the food I selected."

Joy's eyes widened at the last revelation. "I do. It's one of my favorites."

"Good." Luke, looking pleased with himself, pulled out two plastic wine glasses and set them on the table. A wine opener appeared and before she knew it, she was holding a glass of rich, deep wine. What had happened? Was she really in her store, with a spread of delicious food in front of her, and a handsome man to keep her company? Yes, she was.

. . .

Luke gestured that she should eat, so she did. Choosing a little of everything to add to the small paper plate he handed to her. She sipped her wine and ate her food, and felt... relaxed. Which was a wholly unfamiliar sensation during her busiest season. They found more to talk about than she expected and before she realized it, an hour flew by.

"Oh no, I have to tabulate winners still..." she trailed off, glancing at the pile of work awaiting her on the counter.

"Bring them over, we'll do it together. Share the work."

She glanced at him sideways. "You want to work on this with me?"

He grinned that sexy grin of his. "Well, who else will?"

The answer was no one. Until this year, when she volunteered him, mostly to be spiteful, no-one helped her. She was a judging committee of one. She had to admit this wasn't the worst way to judge. With someone else, over food and wine. This was a one-time thing, though, she reminded herself. Not something to get used to. Next year, it would be back to her and her alone. The way she liked it. Right?

Luke had no idea what he was doing. It wasn't like him to bring dinner to a woman he didn't even particularly like. Who was supposed to be his arch-rival. Which sounded a little dramatic. But there it was. Somehow, though, Luke found himself sitting in a cozy corner of a Christmas store, sorting ballots. He did not do cozy, nor Christmas, nor community. Yet, here he was. With a sigh, he popped an olive in his mouth while Joy considered the finer points of a holiday display. Their tallying had resulted in a three-way tie and she was debating which house would win. To be fair, they were all amazing and worthy of the win. He wasn't sure why it mattered who won, really since the honor seemed just that, an honor. The cash prize was enough to buy dinner out, at best.

Still, Joy agonized over the scoring as if the stakes were much higher. He had to appreciate that about her. She seemed to care about her community. A lesser person, like him, would have picked a winner at random and moved on with his life. Joy, on the other hand, went through each finalist's strengths carefully, weighing one against the other. She had finally narrowed it down to two.

"Luke, which would you choose?" Him? Was he the deciding vote? That felt like too much responsibility for someone who didn't care one way or another who won.

"I don't know, Joy. You have more experience with this. Why don't you choose?"

"The whole point of more than one judge is to have a tie-breaker," she reminded him, taking another sip of wine. Maybe it was the food or the wine, but she seemed more relaxed than he had ever seen her. He thought again about their kiss last night. Maybe there was something there, a little spark? It would be a shame to let it pass. He leaned closer, resting his arms on his knees. Closer to Joy, he could smell her perfume, something soft and sweet like the woman herself.

Her lips were pursed as she studied her scoring sheets and he had the urge to kiss her again. She held up two papers as he started to lean in.

"Which one?"

Luke tried to focus on the papers, distracted from his goal.

"This one," he chose, pointing to the house with the Mistletoe under the lights. "It was really special." *It was also our first kiss.* That decided, he returned his attention to his task of kissing Joy.

Before he made his move, she stood up and fussed around the small table, collecting garbage and putting away their leftovers. She returned to her seat and relaxed back, closing her eyes.

"I can't relax until the work is done. Now…" she sighed as she raised her arms over her head to stretch, "I can relax."

"I don't know how you do all the things you do." Joy was a machine, running her store and the holiday committee each year. It meant a lot to her. A sharp pain of guilt twisted in his gut. He was a real jerk to kick her out of the store she loved and her home. He couldn't do that to her, after all. Tomorrow, he would call the real estate agent and take the property off the market. He had no idea what he would do with a hundred-year-old building, but he would figure something out. He always did. And, his brother's offer of the job training rodeo horses might be the opportunity he needed right now. As much as he loved the rodeo, he was getting older, as his brothers so tactfully pointed out, and he couldn't keep this pace forever. Maybe returning to Wildwood Falls to settle into steady work wasn't putting himself out to pasture, but enjoying his well-deserved retirement.

Joy opened her eyes, peering at him skeptically. "Who are you and what did you do with Luke?"

Luke laughed, feeling all the weight of the past week's lift. "I'm just feeling the Christmas spirit," he teased with a wink.

"Hmm, the Christmas spirit suits you." Was that appreciation in her eyes? Luke scrubbed his face, feeling the day's stubble. He didn't feel particularly attractive today. And, Joy certainly couldn't be warming up to him. Could she?

She picked up her wine, taking thoughtful sips. "You must miss your Aunt Mary. Especially losing her so close to the holiday."

"Yeah, she was so full of life, I don't think it ever occurred to me she wouldn't live forever."

Joy's smile was wistful. "I know, she had such a big personality. Every time she came into the store, the whole place lit up."

Luke sat up straight. "She came into the store?" He couldn't picture his aunt, an ever-practical rancher's wife, buying frilly ornaments.

"Yes, she came in all the time. She loved to look around at all the displays. And, she hosted the Mrs. Clause read-a-longs. Oh, and helped on the holiday committee, of course."

Luke sat back, trying to process this new information. His Aunt was Mrs. Clause? And served on the holiday commit-tee? How had he not known this? Maybe because he spent as much time away from Wildwood Falls as possible. *What else had he missed out on?*

With a start, he realized that the activities stipulated in the will were not chosen at random. They were some of the activities she did each year. Instead of the silly hoops he had imagined, they were designed so that her role was filled the first holiday after her passing. So the town, and Joy, didn't miss her presence as much. He was a jerk.

"You must miss her, then, very much. I had no idea that you knew her so well. I'm sorry I was so insensitive when we first met."

Eyes filled with tears, Joy nodded. "I do miss her, espe-cially during the holidays. Having your help, though, has filled the hole she left. Thank you for that. No matter what happens in the future, know that I will always be grateful you were here at a time when I needed you."

How often could he say he was needed? Or had been useful? Pretty much never, by his design. This feeling, though, of pride and contentment, while unfamiliar, was welcome. It wasn't the same as the rush of riding a bull and making it to 8 seconds without being trampled, but it was a good feeling. A feeling that, maybe, somewhere inside, he was a good person. Not just a popular person. Or a desired person. But, a good person.

"I'm not going to sell the building."

CHAPTER 9

She must be hearing things. Or the wine must have gotten to her. She thought Luke just said he wasn't selling the building. Which, she knew must be impossible. She very carefully set the wine down on the table.

"What did you say?" She held her breath, waiting for Luke's reply.

"I said I'm not selling the building. I just can't. It's too much a part of the town's history. My family's history. And, holiday traditions. It would be wrong to lose this building."

Impulsively, Joy threw herself into Luke's arms. "Thank you so much. This means so much to me. And, the town. You're doing the right thing." Luke reflexively put an arm around her to steady her on his lap. He returned the hug before gently settling her back on her feet. His cheeks were flushed and his eyes bright. Attraction? Or embarrassment?

Luke shrugged. "My brother offered me a job training rodeo horses at the ranch. I figure I should at least give it a go."

Looking at his watch, he stood abruptly. "It's late. I should be going."

Before she knew it, he was heading out the front door, admonishing her to lock it behind her.

Joy sank back down on the couch and stared at the cheerful fake fireplace. What had just happened? Her rival had just become her…friend? The kiss they shared the night before suggested more than friendship. While the kiss had been amazing, she did not want to start something with a rodeo cowboy who had plans to leave town. A rancher who talked about putting down roots, however, she might consider.

She hesitated to name the feelings flooding her. It was too soon for love. Or was it? She liked Luke, very much. Which was inconvenient when she also hated him very much. Now, there was no reason to be angry with him. The feelings left felt very much like the beginnings of love, which should scare her. But, surprisingly, didn't. She had lived on her own in Montana for a few years now, which was enough time to put the past behind her. All the family struggles and demands to be a certain way and reach a certain level of success in her father's eyes were safely in the past. She felt ready to move into the future.

The immediate future came much too quickly as Joy found herself the next morning, turning the key in the lock, once more, to open the store. The morning was busy and before she knew it, lunch beckoned. She left the store in her assistant's hands and walked two doors down to the cafe on the corner. What a different feeling today, knowing that it would be safe from development into condos. Greeting her friend, Sarah, who owned the cafe, she placed her usual order and sat down, idly flipping through the local paper. Her whole page ad greeted her, reminding her she needed to call the paper and cancel that ad. Now that Luke wasn't selling, there was no need to keep the ad in place.

She wondered what Luke was doing at that moment? Was

he working on the ranch? When would she see him again? They had no business reason to get together. So, it would have to be personal. Joy picked up her phone and typed a quick message. What are you doing tonight? I owe you dinner...

There, that was straightforward and to the point. She put the phone down, trying not to watch for a response.

Within a minute, her phone pinged with a message. Sure, sounds like fun. I'll come by at 7. Joy resisted the urge to squeal like a girl. She was going to see Luke tonight. And, explore what this thing between them was.

"Here's your salad." Joy was pulled from her daydreaming by her lunch.

"Thanks. Want to join me a few?" Sarah looked at the lunchtime crowd, well in hand by her staff.

"Sure, why not? They can get by without me for a few minutes. And, I'm curious what has you looking so dreamy."

Joy felt a flush creep up her cheeks. "I was just thinking of Luke."

"Really? A thousand ways to hurt him?" she asked with a laugh.

"Well, he isn't selling the building after all. He is keeping it."

Sarah looked surprised. "Rodeo cowboy has a heart? There's a plot twist."

"Sarah. Don't be so hard on him. He's a nice guy. I think his conscience finally won out. He said he was taking the property off the market."

"Ok. What's his angle? I've known Luke since school and he's always done what benefits him. I'm not sure he has a conscience."

"This is different," Joy insisted, though a small voice in the back of her mind wondered if she was protesting too much.

"He said he's taking a job with his brothers training rodeo horses. That he's staying in town."

Sarah cocked her head. "Hmm. Maybe love has changed him."

"Love? What does that have to do with anything?"

Sarah laughed. "I heard about that kiss a few nights ago. Don't forget you live in a small town now. Nothing to do but gossip. And, two rivals engaged in a most romantic kiss under the mistletoe during a very public holiday lights stroll is worthy of gossip."

Joy was mortified. The whole town knew about the kiss?

Sarah laughed again. "Joy, it's ok. We've all been there, being the subject of gossip. It means you've become one of us."

One of us. It felt good to be part of something.

Her phone rang and she felt a cold dread when she saw it was from her store. What was wrong? She was up and walking while answering. Her assistant sounded shaken as she said Joy needed to come right away.

Bursting through the door, Joy stood face to face with a commercial realtor.

Luke hummed as he pulled out of the ranch and towards town. He took a lot of teasing from his brothers for his outfit. He wore his best jeans, tightest fitting black tee, and a black cowboy hat. He pulled out the very expensive cowboy boots he bought with his first rodeo win and his largest rodeo buckle. Just because he wanted to look his best didn't mean he was gaga over a girl, as his brothers had suggested. He liked Joy, wanted to see more of her. He couldn't remember the last time he had felt this much excitement over a woman. Or had seen her more than once in a row. He may have decided not to sell the building. And to stay in town to put down roots. That didn't mean he was ready to settle down with a woman. He wouldn't mind getting to know Joy, spend more time with her. She was like no one he had known before and he was intrigued. He was surprised the realtor hadn't called him back yet to ask him to consider changing his mind about taking the property off the market. It meant a loss of commission for the realtor and there was already a buyer expressing serious interest. He made a mental note to call her tomorrow to check in.

As he parked and headed towards Joy's store, he noticed a crowd on the sidewalk. Was there yet another holiday event happening in town tonight?

As he got closer, he realized this was no cheery holiday event. The group could be best described as a mob. A very angry mob. Holding up signs that read Save Our History and Say No To Corporate Sellouts. What was going on?

When he was standing in front of Joy's store, it became apparent the mob was there for him. Why hadn't Joy called off her tribe of supporters? He wasn't selling the building, so no need for demonstrations. He needed to talk to Joy. He was almost at the front door when a tall blond stepped his path. "Nope, Not gonna happen."

Luke cocked his head in confusion. "What is going on?"

The tall blond, Sarah, he remembered, owned the cafe on the corner. "We won't let her go without a fight."

The "her" in question was undoubtedly the building.

"Okayyy. But I'm keeping her. Not selling. Didn't Joy tell you that?"

For a moment, Sarah seemed unsure. Shaking her head, she continued. "You told her you weren't selling, but the next day, a real estate shark showed up on her doorstep to take pictures and measurements for a listing.

Damn. He had left a very clear message. Had the realtor not gotten it?

"I had her scheduled before I talked to Joy. I decided to cancel and I called her. She must not have gotten my message. I wouldn't lie to Joy."

Sarah stepped out of the way. "Well, it's on you if you want to face an angry mob to tell her that yourself. But you may want to talk to her later." She looked around her at the angry group. "When it's quieter."

Luke pressed forward into the group. Waiting wasn't an option. He reached the door of Tinsel & Co and pulled it open to find Joy behind the counter. Her expression didn't change and gave him no clue what she was thinking.

"I canceled the realtor. She didn't get my message."

Joy sighed deeply, sadness clear in her eyes. "I know. She called ten minutes ago to apologize and said she had missed your message."

Luke was relieved. She knew he hadn't lied. Now, they could resolve this thing between them.

"Good. I'm glad you know that I'm a man of my word. I like spending time with you. I'd like to keep seeing you, past the holiday season." Those last words squeaked out like he was a teenage boy. What a risk to put himself out there and risk rejection. He could not remember a time when he had felt like this before. Where his next breath hinged on her answer to his question.

Joy took a deep breath and closed her eyes. "No, Luke. I can't. I can't see you again."

CHAPTER 10

This was both the best and stupidest thing she had ever done all at once. It was the right thing to do, turning him down. Even though he hadn't lied and had braved a mob of angry townspeople to tell her that, Joy couldn't take the risk to get involved with him. The few hours when she had thought he lied were the worst of her life. The sharp betrayal lodged in her chest and wouldn't release, even when she had learned the truth. This was about more than Luke. It was about her. She got too wrapped up in what other people thought of her and got lost in them. She needed a clear and decisive boundary between her and other people. That just wasn't possible with Luke. Her only choice was to walk away. They had only known each other for a few weeks. It was better to end things now before they began, then to get hurt more deeply later.

The hurt that was so clear in Luke's eyes gutted her, but she remained strong. This was for the best. She offered her best forced cheerful smile. "It was nice to get to know you, Luke, but where is this going anyway? You and I are so different. What does a rodeo cowboy have in common with the owner of a Christmas store anyway? You'd get bored soon enough…"

To his credit, Luke only nodded his agreement. For a moment, she thought he'd argue with her, but he didn't. Instead, he smiled a resigned smile.

"I like you, Joy, and I want to be friends at least. I think there could be more, but I can't make you like me if you don't. I respect your decision. Merry Christmas."

With that, he turned and walked away. The bell chimed behind him as he closed the door, the cheery sound in stark contrast with the heaviness in her heart. It was for the best, she reminded herself, her father's voice ringing in her head. *That's not for you, Joy. Don't try to make yourself better than you are.*

She had learned that lesson hard over the years. Don't wish for things you can't have. Don't think you deserve better than you've got. Wanting more only leads to disappointment. Being happy with what you have avoids pain.

Luke swung the hay bale high and threw it in a growing pile in the barn. No time like the present to organize the barn. His work would begin in earnest after New Years, as the new head of training for the horse breeding program. He would be responsible for taking horses from a young age and training them to be stellar rodeo horses. He was happy with his decision to stay in town. Even if things hadn't worked out with Joy. He didn't make a decision based on a woman he knew for two weeks. That would be ridiculous.

His brother, Will, came in as he was hefting the next bale.

"Those hay bales do something to offend you?" Will asked as he leisurely leaned against a post.

"Just straightening up the barn."

"On Christmas eve? That makes perfect sense."

"Well, what else should I be doing?"

"Going to the Christmas eve tree lighting with the rest of us."

"I don't feel much in the holiday spirit at the moment."

Will shrugged. "Suit yourself. You know you can't avoid her forever. You live in the same small town. You're going to see her again. Might as well be now." With that pronouncement, Will headed out of the barn and left Luke to his thoughts.

His brother had it all wrong. He wasn't avoiding her. He just didn't feel much like Christmas Spirit at the moment. He didn't even know if she would be there. *Of course, she'd be there. She was the chair of the holiday committee.* He was a member of the committee, though it didn't matter now that he wasn't selling the building. He wasn't obligated to do any more holiday events. He was free to enjoy his life as he always did. Except something about that rankled. It seemed he didn't want to enjoy his life the way he always did. He wanted to go to the big, bright, and loud holiday tree lighting. And maybe even run into a fair-haired beauty that hated his guts at the moment. Just to see a glimpse of her and make sure she was ok. With a curse, he tossed the last hay bale and headed for his truck. Too late to go with the rest of his family but that was ok. He was a man on a mission and didn't need any distractions.

Luke cursed at the traffic jam on Main St. Apparently, the entire town was attending the lighting. He pulled into the side street and parked in the first parking space he saw. Walking the few blocks to the center of town, he scanned the crowd, looking for Joy. Where was she? She was the chair of the committee. No way she would miss this. He passed the small stage near the tree, which was still empty. The crowd milled around, taking advantage of local vendors who had set up tents for food and hot chocolate. Holiday music played from speakers on the stage. He saw the oversized button that would light up the tree, on a small table on the stage. Ah, that was where the action would occur soon. If he couldn't find Joy in the crowd, she was sure to be on stage at some point during the festivities.

He wasn't sure what he planned to say when he found her. She had heard him out already and had turned him down. He just knew he needed to see her again.

CHAPTER 11

Joy finished her rounds in preparation for the lighting and stood watching the community, her community, enjoying the event. She watched the young couples holding hands and sneaking kisses. And, the families with small children in tow, sipping hot chocolate and laughing. For the first time in a long while, she wanted something she didn't have. That love. Affection. Connection. For a moment, she wondered what could have become of her and Luke. That evening in her store was almost magical. She let her mind wander to imagine evenings by a real fire, sipping wine, and talking about the day. Or kissing. She sighed deeply. That was not meant to be for her and Luke. How could she trust that a relationship would work out when her parents' sure hadn't. Her mother's passive withdrawal and her father's stern warnings were a cautionary tale of what happened when you fell in love without boundaries. She had witnessed what became of love when passion was unrestrained and there were no checks and balances.

She had sworn to herself she wouldn't fall victim to that kind of love. And Luke was temptation down that exact road.

Love without limits, passion with no reins. How could she hold onto herself when the feeling of loving Luke threatened to pull her under. Loving Luke? She paused a moment to consider that idea. Was she in love with Luke? She had never been in love before. Not like this. A part of her was curious about this new awakening while a greater part of her wanted to run as far away as possible. Could she try? Could this thing between them work? The more she thought of Luke, the more she wanted to know. To find out. To give them a chance. She looked around, wondering if he was here some-where. Probably not. Now that he wasn't selling his building, he didn't need to bother with the holiday committee. That had just been a means to an end for him. Though she had liked the company. She hadn't realized how alone she had felt until Luke.

She spotted his brothers gathered around the only tent that served adult beverages. Holding beers, they laughed at their private joke. She didn't see Luke among them. It wouldn't hurt to ask, though, just in case he was around. She wasn't sure what she would say to him if she found him, but just knew she needed to see him again.

The static of the microphone system broke into her thoughts. With a start, she looked at her watch. Was she late? There were still 20 minutes until the tree lighting. She started to move towards the stage. Had teenagers taken over the mic for a prank?

A familiar voice carried over the crowd. "Good evening, ladies and gentlemen. Sorry to interrupt your evening but I have a very important announcement." Luke? What was he doing here? Holding the mic?

She had reached the edge of the crowd, now, and could see him on the stage, faded jeans, old boots, well-worn work jacket. He looked perfect. She held her breath while she waited for him to speak again.

"Has anyone seen Joy? She's the star of this show isn't she?" He scanned the crowd until his gaze landed on her, standing in a pool of light.

"Joy. Thank you for organizing all this." He gestured broadly, taking in the town all lit up for the holidays. "When I was a boy, I remember the magic of the town's holiday celebration. As I grew up, I stopped coming home as often for the holiday. Somehow, I thought magic was only for childhood." He paused to reach his hand down off the stage until she put her hand in his and allowed him to guide her up on stage.

He turned to face her. "Joy, I may not have volunteered my time for the holiday celebration, but you still welcomed me warmly. You've taken a cherished memory of this town and made it even better. Even brighter and more joyful."

She felt her cheeks grow hot under the weight of the town's attention.

"I may not have had the best intentions for this town when I started, but because of you, I realized what holiday tradition means to this community. And to me. I'm part of this community and I plan to be for a good, long time."

Joy nodded, blushing. Feeling tears prick behind her eyes. This was what she had hoped for when she included Luke on the holiday committee. That he would come to see the importance of tradition to this town. She was so glad that he had.

"And, since I plan to be a part of this community for a good long time, I'd like to get to know you better. I know I haven't always been the best man, but I want to do better. I want to be the best man for you, Joy. If you'll give me a chance."

He put the mic down, standing facing her, looking hopeful and so damn handsome. It occurred to Joy that this was the second time he had bared his soul to her. The first, in her store, braving a raging mob to do it. The second, now, in front of the entire town who was here for the holiday tree lighting.

She glanced through the crowd, hearing appreciative murmurs. The town had seemed to find it in their collective hearts to forgive him. Could she?

She met his eyes, smiled a genuine joyful smile, and gave her answer.

"Yes, yes I'll give you a chance."

The last thing she saw before he pulled her in for a kiss was his wide grin as he moved in to claim her for his own Christmas wish.

Want more of Wildwood Falls, Montana? Meet Luke's brother, Cameron, in Sweet on her Favorite Rancher. A preview of chapter one is included on the next page.

Sign up for updates from Heather Scarlett
Heather Scarlett's Reader Group

SWEET ON HER FAVORITE
RANCHER PREVIEW

Alexia Lewis drove up the winding driveway to the Hudson ranch, her stomach in knots. She gripped the steering wheel with sweating palms as she navigated down the dirt road.

The trees surrounding the drive were more mature than they were twelve years ago, when she first visited. The large wooden sign announcing Hudson ranch was a little more weathered. She supposed she was, as well.

Anticipation settled in the pit of her stomach. She took first one sweaty hand, then the other, off the steering wheel to rub them down her shorts.

What would it be like to see Cameron Hudson again after all these years? She smoothed down her long, dark waves. She couldn't risk a check of her appearance in the rearview mirror since she was driving. While May in Montana wasn't hot, the humidity was rough on her curls. She hoped the extra styling products she'd used today did their job.

She parked the car in her usual spot, along the fence line. Though she supposed it wasn't her usual spot anymore.

Funny, though, how the vehicles in the driveway were unfamiliar, but none were in her spot, as if it was waiting for her.

She remained in the car, gazing ahead at the miles of pasture beyond. Sighing, she placed her hands on the steering wheel, then rested her head on them. She took several deep breaths, willing her racing heart to slow.

Memories flooded of times past. This ranch had been a second home to her, even more welcoming than her own in Seattle. She'd first learned to ride a horse on this ranch, sat down with the family for meals, experienced her first kiss, and fallen in love.

A man stood at the tailgate of an oversized pickup, unloading wood. He hefted a large piece onto his shoulder, and Alexia watched with fascination as his biceps bulged and flexed. He was wearing a tight white tee shirt which emphasized his deep tan. A flush spread from her face down her neck and she shivered. *Who was this man?*

Alexia let her gaze travel from his muscled shoulders down past his trim waist to his thick thighs encased in denim. Maybe there would be a silver lining to helping with the wedding if it meant she might get to know this fine specimen.

A final deep breath and appearance check in the rearview mirror, then she pushed open her car door and got out as gracefully as possible while also pretending she was not ogling the sexy man. Wildwood Falls was a small town and there were few people she didn't know as the owner of the only bakery in town. *How had this man escaped her notice?*

She wished she was the kind of woman to just walk right up to a handsome man and say hello. Opportunity didn't strike too often in her experience. She really should take advantage.

Rather than seize the moment, however, she took the

cowardly way out and shifted her gaze away to the barns in the distance. She kicked the toe of her sneaker in the dirt, her hand coming up to absentmindedly twirl a curl.

Heart racing, Alexia debated her next move. Did she go up to the house or should she head for the barn where the wedding would be held? She couldn't awkwardly stand here forever and ignore the stranger. Each moment that ticked past became increasingly uncomfortable.

Before she could decide, the stranger set his load down on the truck bed and made his way over to her. Her skin prickled and her heart threatened to pound out of her chest. *Was it possible to die of anticipation?*

The man approached in long, confident strides and she couldn't help but notice how well he filled out his jeans. The scruff on his jaw gave him a dangerous look. She shivered.

Alexia stood tall, returning her hands to her sides and willing herself to remain in place, even though every instinct said to run. She forced herself to take a deep breath to counter the lightheadedness. Clearly it was possible to die from wanting.

"Alexia?"

She startled at her name, curious how this stranger would know her. She'd have remembered if he came into the bakery.

"Yes, I'm here to work on the wedding favors with Sarah." She silently cursed the squeak in her voice.

"She mentioned that. She's down at the barn. You remember how to get there?" His gaze swept over her, as if he was drinking after a long drought. He swallowed and Alexia watched his adam's apple bob.

"Yes, I do." Alexia studied the man closely. He looked vaguely familiar. Had they met?

His mouth twisted in a wry smile. "I suppose we spent plenty of time down there."

We? Then it clicked. This was Cameron. All grown up and hot as a wildfire.

Alexia's heart stopped, then beat wildly at the realization. She'd expected her reunion with Cameron to be awkward since they hadn't seen each other in years and had never really had any closure to their youthful fling. She had not expected it to be awkward because he was the most attractive man she'd ever seen.

And she'd been salivating over him just moments before. This was not going as expected.

"Thanks, Cameron," she replied. "I'll just head down and find Sarah." And her dignity. What was left of it, at least.

Cameron rubbed the back of his neck as he made a concerted effort to stand upright. Alexia damn near brought him to his knees. She was beautiful at fourteen. She was drop-dead gorgeous now.

He'd known he would see her today. Luke had given him advanced notice of the plan. He'd been prepared. So he thought. There was no way he could have prepared himself for the gut punch that was Alexia all grown up. She'd stood in the dirt, gazing at the pastures, seeming nervous. Then, she'd turned those green eyes on him and he was nearly struck down where he stood. The look of pure attraction rooted him to the spot. It was a wonder he found his voice.

He was tempted to rush to her, pick her up, and spin her in his arms. That had been their standard greeting. It had been seven years, though, so he held back. As he watched Alexia make her way down to the barn, he was reminded of the many times in the past they'd make that trip together. Holding hands, laughing, kissing.

He shook his head, hoping to shake thoughts of Alexia

from his memory. He'd been playing their past on an endless loop in his head since she'd left for the last time at nineteen. And even more since she'd returned. He'd worked hard to avoid her since her return, which was an impressive feat in a small town. The fact that he avoided her for almost a year deserved some kind of prize.

Self-protection drove his avoidance. One which was validated the moment he saw her step out of the car. Long legs in denim cutoffs and a snug tank top. Her dark waves framed her face and tumbled around her shoulders. An image of her hair spread out on the grass as they star-gazed arose, unbidden. He shook it off. It was no secret to him he still had feelings for his first love. He'd like to keep the secret safe from her.

He'd hoped she'd look him up and reconnect when she moved to Wildwood Falls. He's spun fantasies of them confessing their undying love to each other over a reunion dinner. That wasn't to be. She hadn't reached out. So, he avoided her. Obviously, their fling meant more to him than to her.

Cameron entered the barn and dropped his load of wood next to his workspace. Alexia and Sarah were on the other side of the building, near where the wedding supplies were being prepared. His brother, Luke, was marrying the love of his life, Joy, in a few weeks. The women hadn't noticed him come in. Alexia stood next to the arch he was carving as a wedding gift, her fingers tracing the details of the wood.

"This is beautiful," she breathed.

Sarah nodded her agreement. "It is. Cameron does amazing work."

"This is Cameron?!" He was stunned by the wonder evident in Alexia's voice. "It is. I always tell him he should sell his work, but he doesn't. He's too talented to hide his work away in a barn." Cameron never understood when his family make these remarks. To him, his wood carving was a hobby. It got his mind of things. Simple as that.

"He is," Alexia agreed. "I had no idea he did this kind of work. I thought he worked the ranch."

"Oh, he does. The woodworking is in his spare time. Joy says that Luke encourages him to make a living with wood, too. William can always hire extra help for the ranch. And their brother, Dylan, plans to stay here, too."

Cameron bristled at Sarah announcing his business. How did she even know that? He supposed Luke talked to his fiancé and Joy must have shared with her friends. His back muscles tensed at the thought. Did his family sit around talking about his life behind his back? Even though he knew they meant well, the thought rankled.

He turned to sneak out of the barn before he was noticed. As he began to leave, he caught the edge of his hammer and it clattered to the floor. He cursed under his breath. So much for a silent exit.

"Cameron!" Sarah called. "We were just talking about you. Come over and say hi to Alexia. She's here to help."

"I've already said hi," Cameron grunted, admonishing himself for how childish that sounded. He stayed put, neither leaving nor approaching the women. A year of avoiding Alexia, and now he couldn't escape her company.

Given his reaction to her outside, he wasn't sure he was ready to face her again so soon. His mind was a riot of thoughts and he felt emotionally wrung out. He needed some time to think. Alone.

He sighed deeply, resigned that he needed to join them, however briefly. It was not in his nature to be rude, even though it was tempting in this moment. Cameron walked over to Alexia and Sarah, pasting a smile on his face and hoping Alexia wouldn't notice the effect she had on him.

"How's the wedding planning?" He had a pretty good idea

given his proximity to the operation, but it was a neutral topic of conversation.

"Great! We finally got all the favors in and are assembling today. It's going to take a while. Griffin is helping Luke with some ranch work, then they'll grill up a feast. You should come by for dinner."

Cameron didn't point out that he lived here and, therefore, was always here for dinner. It was good to know that Alexia would also be there. He might have to change his plans and head to town. Although now that he had an official invite, that might look suspicious. He didn't want Alexia to know he was avoiding her. Hurting her was the last thing he wanted to do.

"I just may do that. I'm not one to turn down good barbecue." Or the craft beer that would likely be available, also, from the new brewery in town. The space had been a brewpub and events center for some time, but recently was purchased by an out-of-town investor who was well known in the San Diego beer scene. No one had met the mystery brewer yet, but the beer was incredible.

"You're staying too, Alexia?" Sarah asked her friend.

"Um, I may have to check something at the bakery…."

"I thought it was closed Mondays?" Sarah focused her sharp gaze on Alexia, who squirmed.

"Oh, well, I guess it can wait. I'll stay." Seems like Alexia was also trying to avoid him. He should be relieved by that knowledge, but instead it made his skin prickle. He shifted from one foot to the other, as he glanced towards the open barn door.

Sarah frowned as she looked between Cameron and Alexia. Finally, she nodded. "Ok, then. I guess we'll get to work. Fair warning, there is plenty of girl talk planned, so you may want to make yourself scarce."

Cameron didn't need to be told twice. He headed out of

the barn to the safety of the farthest pasture. Checking fence line was preferable to being close to Alexia. Hopefully hard labor would clear his head, so he could get his emotions in check.

Keep reading in Sweet on her Favorite Rancher

ABOUT THE AUTHOR

Heather Scarlett lives in Southern California, although her heart is in Montana where she lived for six wonderful years. She loves big sky, wide open spaces, and cowboys. Heather writes smart and sexy small-town romance that is equal parts sweet and emotionally satisfying. Her heroines are strong and sassy and her heroes are rugged and capable. Heather's stories are family focused and relationship driven.